MOUNTAIN **LION**

TEXT BY REBECCA L. GRAMBO

PHOTOGRAPHS BY DANIEL J. COX

MOUNTAIN LION

CHRONICLE BOOKS

SAN FRANCISCO

BOOK AND COVER DESIGN: STUART MCKEE

COVER PHOTOGRAPH: DANIEL J. COX

DISTRIBUTED IN CANADA BY

RAINCOAST BOOKS

8680 CAMBIE STREET VANCOUVER, B.C.

V6P 6M9

10 9 8 7 6 5 4 3 2 1

CHRONICLE BOOKS

85 SECOND STREET

SAN FRANCISCO, CALIFORNIA 94105

WWW.CHRONICLEBOOKS.COM

PRINTED IN HONG KONG.

LIBRARY OF CONGRESS CATALOGING-IN-
PUBLICATION DATA:

COX, DANIEL J., 1960-
MOUNTAIN LION / PHOTOGRAPHS BY DANIEL J.
COX : TEXT BY REBECCA L. GRAMBO
P.   CM.
INCLUDES BIBLIOGRAPHICAL REFERENCES
AND INDEX.
ISBN 0-8118-1930-2 (PBK.)
1. PUMAS   I. GRAMBO, REBECCA L. (REBECCA
LYNN), 1963- II. TITLE
QL737.C23C686 1999 98-3760
5999.75'24—DC21   CIP

MY CLOSEST FRIEND. WITHOUT HIS HELP THIS

BOOK WOULD NOT EXIST. AND A SPECIAL DEDICATION

TO TROY'S INSPIRATION, DICK O'LEARY.

—D.J.C.

FOR TROY HYDE

A WONDERFUL, GIFTED PERSON

WHO MAKES MY WORLD, AND THAT OF MANY OTHERS,

A MUCH BETTER PLACE.

—R.L.G.

FOR MY SISTER JANE

CONTENTS

ACKNOWLEDGMENTS

I wish to thank Dan Cox for giving me the honor of writing the text to accompany his superb images. And to his wife, Julie, who took time from the hectic job of running their business to answer a thousand and one questions, thank you for your patience and sense of humor. Thank you also to Bill LeBlond and Lesley Bruynesteyn at Chronicle for their enthusiasm and editorial skills, and to Martin G. Jalkotzy of Arc Wildlife Services for graciously finding time to review the manuscript. Any errors remaining in the text are, of course, mine.

Many, many people at various government agencies took time to help me in my quest for facts. Without exception, they went out of their way to be polite, informative, and encouraging. Special thanks to Dennis Jordan of the U.S. Fish and Wildlife Service for taking time to share information on the Florida panther, to John Hervert at the Arizona Game and Fish Department for explaining the Yuma puma situation, and to Michael Dunbar at the National Wildlife Health Center for answering my questions about current research on estrogenic compounds.

Closer to home, Cathryn and David Miller once again demonstrated their exceptional proofreading talents and even provided meals when things got really hectic. As always, my sister and my husband's family supplied encouragement and support. My husband, Glen, went above and beyond the call of duty, taking over many small but time-consuming jobs to give me time to research and write. The other helper in my immediate family, my big rabbit, Teddy, periodically provided amusing distractions by violently rearranging or consuming my research materials. I am happy to report that she remains blissfully ignorant of mountain lions despite the information she has digested.

—R.L.G.

Intelligence, grace, and above all, great latent power—those are the lingering impressions a mountain lion leaves. When the cat's gaze locks with yours, you experience a definite feeling of contact with a presence, of being noted and considered. When you watch a mountain lion move, you see no wasted motion, only an elegant fluidity. But it is the implied strength in the heavily muscled forepaws and haunches that draws your attention again and again.

Mountain lions are solely American predators, occupying habitats from the southern tip of South America all the way up through British Columbia. Wherever they make their home, all healthy mountain lions have a few things in common: they have or wish to have a home range, they hunt for a living, and they find mates and raise families. In this book, we focus on mountain lions living in North America, where, except for the occasional jaguar that makes its way northward, they are the largest of our native cats.

Often the subject of wilderness legends, mountain lions stalk the darkness in countless campfire tales. Until recently, myths about mountain lions far outnumbered the known facts. The reclusive nature of mountain lions makes it difficult to observe them for any length of time in the wild. However, dedicated researchers have spent countless hours studying both wild and captive mountain lions, slowly uncovering the day-to-day lives of these remarkable creatures.

To give you an intimate view of a mountain lion's life, we worked mainly with captive-bred mountain lions under controlled conditions. Much of the time we were with the cats without any fences or enclosures, which allowed them to behave as much like free-roaming mountain lions as possible. This permitted us to see and photograph behaviors and physical details nearly impossible to capture in wild animals without harassing them or endangering ourselves: the way the broad shoulder blades swing smoothly as the cat moves; the extraordinarily rough surface of the bright pink tongue; the attitude of the tail when the cat is relaxed, curious, or angry; the incredible sight of a newborn mountain lion gasping for its first breath while still in its amniotic sac.

They are magnificent creatures, these lions. They deserve our respect and understanding. This book will allow you to share the mountain lions' world for a brief time and, in the process, learn more about them. By doing our best to replace myths and half-truths with carefully collected data, and by appreciating how mountain lions fit into our world, we can make better decisions about the value of mountain lions and their place in our future.

13

A set of tracks on a windswept Patagonian beach signals its presence. In British Columbia, a sinuous figure slips quickly across a logging road. A feral hog in southern Florida snuffles in the lush foliage, unaware that it is being stalked. High in the Rocky Mountains, a tawny form picks its path along the jumbled base of a talus slope. The stars in the clear desert sky of Arizona give enough light for a pair of pale green eyes to see their way.

Incredibly adaptable, mountain lions *(Puma concolor)* live in habitats as varied as rainforest and desert, from sea level to alpine heights—a range covering one hundred degrees of latitude and unmatched by any wild mammal in the Western Hemisphere. At one time their domain stretched from northern British Columbia to southern Chile and Argentina, and from the Atlantic to the Pacific. Today, mountain lions still live throughout Central and South America, but in North America, decades of habitat loss, predator control, and sport hunting have greatly reduced their confirmed range. Now, with the exception of Florida's thirty to fifty cats, only Mexico,

the twelve western U.S. states, and the two western Canadian provinces can confidently claim resident mountain lions. Sightings of the cats have been reported elsewhere, most notably in the Canadian provinces of Saskatchewan, Manitoba, and New Brunswick, but whether these animals are part of a year-round population or merely passing through is still uncertain.

CALLING THE CAT BY NAME

Mountain lion, panther, cougar, puma—the animal has names as diverse as the habitats it occupies. More than eighty variations are recorded. The original human co-inhabitants of the mountain lion's lands had their own names for the cat, including *igmutanka* (Sioux), *mitzli* (Aztec), *ingronga* (Osage), and *yutin* (Apache). In 1500 along the coast of Nicaragua, Amerigo Vespucci made the first recorded sighting of the cat by a European. He believed it to be a lion, as did Columbus when, in 1502, he noted the presence of "leones" in the same general area. The first sighting of a North American mountain lion by a

European didn't occur until 1513, when Alvar Nuñez Cabeza de Vaca spied one in the Florida Everglades. Like Columbus, the explorers who followed compared the animal to those they knew, calling it *tigre rojo* (red tiger), deer tiger, and panther. Cougar is a bastard appellation, being the attempt by Comte de Buffon, a sixteenth-century French naturalist, to simplify what he incorrectly believed to be the Brazilian name for the cat, *cuguacuarana.* Puma, perhaps the most historically pure of all the cat's names, is believed to have been

15

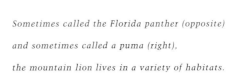

Sometimes called the Florida panther (opposite)
and sometimes called a puma (right),
the mountain lion lives in a variety of habitats.

adopted into the Spanish language as a phonetic approximation of the original Inca name for the animal. Today, in the western regions of North America, both mountain lion and cougar are used, while in the east, panther (sometimes corrupted by regional dialect to painter) is more common. Puma may be heard in the southwestern United States. It's not just the mountain lion's common names that are confusing. The cat even has two Latin names— *Puma concolor* was adopted by the Society

of Mammologists in 1993, but the older, more well known *Felis concolor* is also still in use. While mountain lion, lion, cougar, and puma are used interchangeably for the species as a whole, in this book we will use the name mountain lion, except when referring to Florida mountain lions, which are known as panthers.

EVOLUTIONARY HISTORY

Our understanding of cat family history is based on fossils. Because this fragmentary record may be construed in several different ways, the exact evolutionary path leading to the mountain lion is unclear, but scientists do have a general idea of its origin. About forty million years ago, both the *Felidae* (cat family) and *Canidae* (dog family) split off from the weasel-like, tree-dwelling miacids that lived in the forests of the Northern Hemisphere. Carnivore specialist R. F. Ewer speculates that the *Felidae* evolved from miacids that lived in habitats with good cover, where stalking prey was more likely to be successful than chasing it.

The cats diversified into a variety of species, including the ancestors of mountain lions, who lived in North America from three million to one million years ago. Mountain lions as we know them today first appeared no more than one hundred thousand years ago and have no living close relatives. As mountain lion populations living in various geographic ranges continued to evolve, they developed slightly different physical characteristics. Today most scientists break *Puma concolor* into twenty-six subspecies based on these physical differences, including the Florida panther *(P. c. coryi)*. This number may change when genetic studies currently under way determine whether the Yuma puma *(P. c. browni)* is truly a distinct subspecies.

CAT OF ONE COLOR

The mountain lion is a long, sleek, muscular animal. It appears thin and flat-sided, and its chest is narrow. It may stand two feet or more at the shoulder and an inch or two taller than that in the rear because

Rearing up on its muscular hindquarters, a mountain lion uses its tail to help maintain its balance.

of its powerful hindquarters. Its elegant tail, which makes up about a third of the mountain lion's total length, is cylindrical and about the thickness of a child's arm. From the tip of its tail to the end of its nose, a male mountain lion may measure six to eight feet. Females are smaller, averaging five to seven feet. The mountain lion's former name, *Felis concolor,* translates as "cat of one color," which is a fitting description of any single adult mountain lion. However, while each individual cat is

mainly a single color with a creamy underside, coat color varies throughout the species. Many different words have been used to describe an adult mountain lion's coat: red, buff, tawny, gray, yellow, russett, cinnamon, slate gray, terra cotta, white, pink, orange, black. Cubs have a spotted coat that looks nothing like the adults'.

In North America, black mountain lions are an enigma. There have been reports of them since the first European explorations of the Americas, but although a couple of dark gray or black mountain lions have been documented in South America, no North American sighting has ever been confirmed. One theory about the sightings is that the eastern name, panther, suggests a black animal to most people and that they see what they expect to see. The true black panther, actually a color phase of the leopard, is usually found in the most tropical parts of the leopard's range. Other tropical and subtropical cats, including the jaguar, whose range overlaps the mountain lion's, also sometimes produce black individuals. At one time, jaguars were found

as far north as South Carolina, which might explain some of the earliest sightings. More recently, ten black bobcats, possible candidates for mistaken identity, have come from one small area in south Florida. A black bobcat from New Brunswick widens the geographic possibilities for confusion. However, until a pelt or living specimen is produced and examined by qualified authorities, the black mountain lion of North America will have to remain classified as a myth.

HOME RANGES

An adult mountain lion has an established area, its home range, within which it lives and hunts. Mountain lion home ranges are large, varying from eight square miles to more than four hundred square miles for females, and from twenty-five to five hundred square miles for males. Home range size varies with the time of year, the availability of prey, and the presence of vegetation that feeds prey and provides stalking cover for the mountain lion. The time of year can act as a partial control on the other two variables. Depending on the season, prey may move into or out of an area, and the vegetation may be markedly different. In an area where game is plentiful and there is an abundance of cover, a mountain lion can obtain enough food in a smaller home range than it would require in a more barren environment.

Male and female mountain lions seem to follow different rules in their home range organization. Male home ranges don't often overlap, but the range of one male often overlaps those of several females. Female home ranges sometimes overlap each other, and the boundaries between them appear to change with the number and size of young for which each female is providing.

Resident mountain lions, those in possession of a home range, quite often hold onto it for life. When a resident dies, the vacant range is usually either quickly claimed by a transient mountain lion seeking to establish its own home range, or used by neighboring residents; sometimes a combination of these two scenarios occurs. It is when ownership of a range is being established that hostile, even fatal encounters between mountain lions are most likely to occur.

Mountain lion home ranges are not, strictly speaking, territories, since they have no well-defined borders that are defended against other members of the species. Instead, boundaries between adjacent ranges are somewhat flexible and encroachment by neighboring mountain lions is common and usually tolerated, particularly if direct encounters are avoided. Males, however, are less tolerant than females, sometimes killing other mountain lions caught trespassing. A mountain lion usually avoids wasting valuable time and energy defending its turf by letting other mountain lions know its whereabouts. As it travels throughout its home range, a mountain lion advertises its presence by leaving feces and urine. These tell adjacent residents and passing transients not only that the area is occupied but how recently the owner passed by, allowing the mountain lions to minimize direct contact with one another. The saddles of ridges and the bases of particularly large trees are common places for these scent signs and

19

may be used by more than one mountain lion. Males also leave scrapes, piles of dirt and debris that they pull together with their paws, throughout their home range as signs of occupation. They will sometimes, but not always, mark a scrape with feces or urine. Females appear to make scrapes less often than males.

The driving force behind this elaborate system of marking home range ownership is simple survival. A mountain lion that possesses a home range has a far

greater chance of staying alive than one that does not. This is because while a resident mountain lion is familiar with the land in which it is hunting and with the habits of the prey that lives there, a transient mountain lion, which may still be developing its hunting skills, is constantly dealing with new terrain and unknown hazards. In the precarious day-to-day existence of a carnivore, knowledge and experience often make the difference between life and death.

THE SHAPE OF A HUNTER

Suppose you were given the task of designing a highly efficient carnivore. What qualities would be essential? Such an animal must be able to find prey at a distance, track it, stalk it, and complete the attack with accuracy. Once meat is obtained, the carnivore must be able to process it easily. The mountain lion has evolved to do all of these things with exceptional skill and efficiency.

The mountain lion's sense of smell and hearing are both good, but its exceptional eyesight is its primary tool for locating prey. This is a noticeable difference from members of the dog family, who rely heavily on their noses to find food. I have observed several mountain lions who were unable, purely by smell, to locate bits of meat that had been tossed near them. When they actually saw the meat fall, they were much more successful. Large eyes placed close together at the front of the mountain lion's head provide overlapping fields of view, known as binocular vision, which permit accurate depth perception. The mountain lion's fields of total and binocular vision are both much larger than ours, and its depth perception, always excellent, functions best at between fifty and eighty feet. This allows a stalking mountain lion to very accurately judge its nearness to prey. The rear surface of a mountain lion's eye has a reflective layer, the tapetum lucidum, that directs light back toward the light-gathering part of the eye. Although mountain lions are sometimes active during the day, the advantage provided by the tapetum allows them to hunt from dusk to dawn, their preferred time.

Additional sensory input, very important to an animal active mainly in low light, comes from the mountain lion's whiskers or vibrissae. They send its brain signals that help with close-up spatial orientation— for example, maneuvering through dense brush. The mountain lion uses its sense of hearing, rotating its ears forward and backward, to gather yet more information. This habit is especially noticeable in a resting mountain lion—the cat may remain motionless with its eyes closed, but its ears continually adjust position to monitor

its surroundings. A stalking mountain lion tends to keep its ears pointed forward to focus, like its eyes, on its prey.

Solidly set into the skull, the heavy-boned lower jaw of the mountain lion doesn't move backward or forward, allowing it to absorb the punishing shock of a biting attack. The mountain lion's strong teeth are those of a stereotypical carnivore, designed for piercing and tearing flesh: it possesses a pair of pointed fangs that can be as long as one and one-half inches and

special sharp-edged molars called carnassials. The muscles of the jaw and neck are well developed to allow the mountain lion to bite its prey, hold on to it, and eventually pull away pieces of meat. Any bits of flesh remaining on the bone can be removed by the mountain lion's tongue, which is a bigger, more abrasive version of that belonging to a house cat. The large shreds of meat, torn by the carnassials rather than chewed, are processed by a relatively short digestive tract, typical of animals that are almost exclusively carnivorous.

The strongest evidence of the mountain lion's carnivorous lifestyle can be seen in its forelegs. Massive, rippling with muscles, ending in large paws tipped with retractable crescent-shaped claws, the mountain lion's front legs are designed for holding and bringing down game. Like a house cat, the mountain lion often sharpens its claws on trees or rocks, repeatedly reaching out and then pulling its paws back toward its body along its chosen scratching post. When not in use, the claws are drawn back into sheaths that keep them from being blunted. Each rear paw has four toes,

while each front paw has five, the fifth a dewclaw above the paw on the inside of each foreleg. The underside of the paw has a soft central pad as well as toe pads, and between these pads grows thick hair—the secret behind the mountain lion's ability to walk with ghost-like silence.

When a stalking mountain lion coils into a crouch, its supple spine stores energy that is released when the cat springs forward, propelled by the powerful muscles of its hindquarters. The last bit of mountain lion, its tail, acts as a counterbalance when the cat is jumping, running, and climbing. After studying the mountain lion from nose to tail, it would be difficult to name a more complete and elegant example of a carnivore.

HUNTING TECHNIQUE

The mountain lion's relatively small lungs are not designed for supplying the large amounts of oxygen that long-distance running requires. It has evolved to rely on stealth rather than endurance when hunting. Although many books and movies have

portrayed the mountain lion leaping down onto its victim from a tree branch or rocky ledge, this probably doesn't happen very often, because the odds of being injured would be greatly increased for a cat adopting this tactic. The actual hunting technique of the mountain lion is far more practical, though every bit as exciting.

After scenting, hearing, or seeing prey, the mountain lion adopts a crouching, slow-motion stalk that would be familiar to anyone who has watched the family cat

sneaking up on sparrows. The challenge is to get close enough to the prey to attack before being spotted. Once the prey is within range, the mountain lion launches its final attack with a tremendous forward lunge, powered by the thrust from those great hindquarter muscles. It may take several leaps to reach the target. Then, depending on the size of the prey animal, one of two things happens.

If the animal is small, like a snowshoe hare, one massive front paw deals it a blow that will probably snap its spine immediately. If the animal is larger, the mountain lion usually attacks from the side, reaches out with both forepaws, claws extended, and gets a solid grip on the animal's neck and shoulders. Although the impact of this attack may be enough to break the animal's neck, the mountain lion usually also bites into the back of the neck, forcing its long, slender canines between the vertebrae and severing the spinal cord. If the animal is very large, such as a bull elk, or if the mountain lion is inexperienced, the cat may transfer its bite to the front of the neck and kill its prey by asphyxiation.

Some authorities disagree with this scenario, stating that mountain lions use asphyxiation on all sizes of prey and that it is far more often the cause of death than a broken neck. Killing by asphyxiation takes longer and exposes the mountain lion to possible injury from the victim's flailing hooves. The larger and more powerful the prey, the greater the potential risk to the hunter—many mountain lions have paid for an imperfect attack with their lives.

Once a kill is made, a mountain lion will often rest for a bit before feeding. Then it will use its teeth and tongue to pluck the hair from the area where it wishes to make an opening in the carcass, which it does with its teeth and claws. The mountain lion usually eats the highly nutritious heart, liver, and lungs first. When it has consumed these, it will usually move on to the meat of the hindquarters, and finally to the remainder of the carcass. A hungry adult male may eat nearly twenty pounds of meat. After eating its fill, the mountain lion uses its front paws to rake dirt, snow, grass, leaves, sticks, or other convenient debris over the remaining carcass, perhaps in an effort to hide it from scavengers between meals. Then, retiring to a suitably concealed location nearby, the cat grooms itself and rests, much as a human would after a heavy meal. If not disturbed, mountain lions may feed on the same kill for several days, especially in colder weather. Some researchers think mountain lions are less likely to keep feeding on the same carcass in warm weather because they dislike spoiled meat, but others have observed them feeding on rotting, scavenged carcasses even though they were quite capable of killing for themselves.

DIET

Moose, elk, bighorn sheep, pronghorn, armadillo, beaver, marmot, raccoon, rabbit, various small rodents, and assorted birds—these are just some of the more than thirty kinds of prey North American mountain lions are known to eat. Deer are probably their most common prey, but mountain lions are opportunistic feeders, taking advantage of whatever prey is abundant in their home range. For example, where mule deer are plentiful, such as in Utah, they may make up 80 percent of a mountain lion's diet, whereas Florida panthers, who also dine on deer, eat the local white-tailed variety and add feral hogs to their menu. Another factor in the choice of prey is personal preference. One Arizona mountain lion was observed to eat mostly porcupines even though deer were plentiful in its home range.

Mountain lions sometimes kill and eat other mountain lions, but this is probably a result of a confrontation over home range possession, rather than motivated by hunger. Mountain lions sometimes eat domestic stock, particularly sheep and calves, which brings them into direct conflict with humans. Some individual cats make domestic livestock a major part of their diet, but the majority of mountain lions eat very few, if any, domestic animals.

How much food a mountain lion requires varies depending on whether it is a solitary cat or a female with young to feed. For example, a study in southern Utah showed that, on average, a solitary female killed one deer every sixteen days while a female providing for three fifteen-month-old cubs killed a deer every three days.

RAISING A FAMILY

The solitary nature of the mountain lion is overcome by its drive to reproduce. The animals, which are sexually mature by the time they are two years old, can mate at any time of the year, but each region has some months when mating is more common.

25

Female mountain lions may delay breeding until they have attained the security of an established home range. Mountain lions ready to mate must first find each other in miles of rugged terrain. They are aided by the fact that male and female home ranges partially overlap and also by the fact that the female's urine appears to carry subtle signals that reveal her readiness to mate. Male mountain lions apparently spend much of their time searching for females in heat. Consequently, most mating happens in the female's home range, after a male successfully locates her. Both mountain lions become more vocal at this time, producing a louder version of an amorous domestic cat's caterwauling yowl.

The timing of the meeting between male and female is crucial, because the female is receptive for only a limited number of days each month. Even then, she seems less than thrilled with the entire process, often responding to the male's first advances with hissing snarls and extended claws. Eventually, she allows the male to mount, and breeding takes place quickly, lasting about a minute. This is not the end of the relationship, however: as long as the female remains receptive, the mountain lions may couple a remarkable fifty to seventy times a day. They typically continue this for three to four days; some pairs have been observed to persist for twice as long. Researchers theorize that this behavior may serve to stimulate ovulation or to prove the male's fitness to the female.

Once the female's receptive period ends, the male and female mountain lions part company and resume their separate lives. At this point, many different things can happen. Information gathered by researchers gives us a picture of how an average mountain lion raises her family.

Mountain lions have a gestation period of eighty-eight to ninety-six days. At the end of this time, the female retires to a simple den that may be in the midst of a dense thicket, under an uprooted tree, in the jumbled mess of a boulder pile or rock slide, or even in the trunk of a hollow tree. Dens vary according to habitat; the only general rule governing them seems to be that they must offer a clear line of vision and escape while affording the cubs

some protection from the elements. Inside this minimal shelter, the female mountain lion gives birth to anywhere from one to six cubs. If she is a first-time mother, she is more likely to have a single cub, but the average litter size is two or three.

Only ten inches long, weighing less than a pound apiece, and scarcely able to lift their heads, newborn mountain lion cubs are blind and helpless. With their spotted coats and pointy, ringed tails, they bear little resemblance to their parents. The

cubs suckle greedily soon after birth, their small paws kneading their mother's teats. The milk provided by their mother has a much higher fat content than that of humans and helps the cubs to grow quickly.

In their first two weeks of life, the cubs double their weight. Their blue eyes open and they begin to make their first wobbly explorations of the den area. Their mother may have already moved them to a new location, carrying each cub by the scruff of its neck. Mountain lion families

often change dens several times, which may be one reason that their dens are not more elaborate. The female mountain lion leaves her young cubs alone only when she needs to hunt. Small and vulnerable, they could easily fall victim to a predator, including their own father. Barring mishaps, the cubs continue to grow rapidly, and at five weeks of age, they are chubby bundles of energy bent on detailed investigation of their surroundings.

The mountain lion cubs' long journey toward independence starts with their first meal of meat. It marks the beginning of their weaning and signals that they will soon be accompanying their mother on hunts. The female mountain lion brings her cubs their first taste of meat when they are about six weeks old. She drags a recent kill, or part of one, to the den and carefully licks away its hair to expose some flesh. Then she moves away and watches. At first, the cubs have no idea what to do and may even be afraid of the carcass. They often attack it or play with an ear or tail. But eventually they find the bare meat and begin to gnaw. When the cubs are finished,

their mother grooms them, licking away the blood from their paws and muzzles.

The act of grooming seems to be pleasurable and reassuring for both mother and cubs. When she returns from hunting, the female greets her cubs with short, squeaky meows and a few licks. After nursing them, she uses her rough tongue, capable of rasping meat from bone, to gently wash each cub. She often gives a rumbling purr throughout the process, and the cubs tolerate licks that sometimes tumble them off their feet.

Besides the care she takes in grooming her cubs, the female mountain lion displays remarkable patience with them, enduring playful assaults on her head and tail, and only occasionally administering a swat to a too-aggressive cub. This forbearance is sorely tested, because mountain lion cubs do a great deal of playing. They stalk invisible birds, sneak up on and attack each other, and, in general, act much like any other kittens. Aside from the exercise they provide, these games serve a very important purpose, developing skills that the cubs will eventually need to survive on their own.

When they are four-and-a-half months old, the cubs begin to lose their baby spots and their eyes start to change from blue to pale golden-green. Their baby teeth are soon replaced by permanent ones as they continue the transformation from fuzzy baby to adult mountain lion. At ten months, the cubs are nearly two-thirds the size of their mother. Only the faintest remnants of their baby spots are visible, but the dark apostrophes over their eyes remain, giving them a quizzical look. The cubs may sometimes hunt independently at this stage, venturing off on their own after small prey like rabbit or ground squirrel, but they still rely on their mother to provide bigger game.

Mountain lion cubs mature more slowly than many animals, some remaining with their mother for as long as two years, although most leave after about eighteen months. The mother eventually becomes less welcoming to her offspring, gradually increasing her aggressiveness until they leave to find territories of their own. Because of the prolonged care period, a female mountain lion raises a litter only once every year and a half to two years. However, if her cubs should die, the female will soon come back into heat again.

The natural hazards of life for any wild predator include injury and disease. Reaching its tenth birthday would be quite a feat for a wild mountain lion, although they have occasionally lived twice that long in captivity.

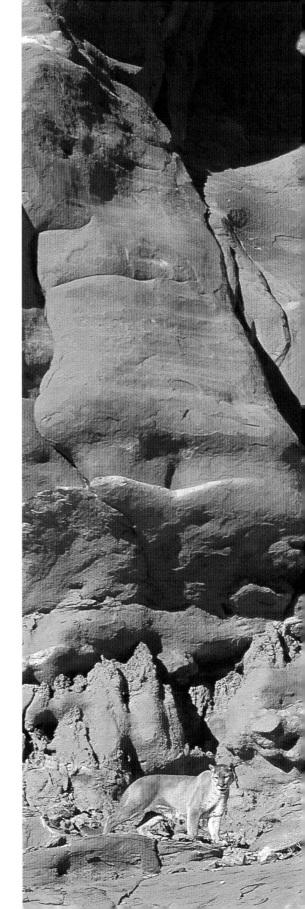

HUMANS AND MOUNTAIN LIONS

Like most predators, mountain lions bring out the extremes in human beliefs. They are worshiped or hated, gods or devils—and to some people they even manage to be both. Perhaps what is most confusing about this dichotomy is that mountain lions are admired and despised for the same quality—their great prowess as hunters.

BELIEFS OF THE NATIVE PEOPLES

The Chickasaws called the mountain lion *Koe-Ishto* or *Ko-icto,* "the Cat of God."

To the Cherokees, it was *Kandaghi,* "Lord of the Forest." The Zuñi people named it *Hâ' k-ti tä' sh-a-na,* "Long Tail," and it was the master of all their prey gods. The Hopis considered it a guardian of their tribe. The Mixtec people of Mexico claimed one as their ancestor. And to the native people of California, who followed vultures to the mountain lion's kills, it was a provider of essential food. To all of these people, the mountain lion was an object of veneration.

However, many people had mixed feelings about the cat. The Pueblos, who like the Zuñis saw the mountain lion as the greatest of all hunters, also considered it an enemy. A man who killed one was admitted to the warrior society just as if he had killed a human foe. The Potawatami people, and others, conjured up a fierce monster called the Underwater Panther, a strange creature with the body and tail of a mountain lion, a deer's antlers, snake scales, feathers from birds of prey, and an assortment of parts from other animals. This frightening beast lived in bodies of water and could call up storms capable of

swamping frail canoes or flooding shoreline villages. The Underwater Panther had a benevolent side as well, though, sometimes depositing lumps of shining copper on the shore. The Incas, who placed treasonous or disobedient prisoners in dungeons with mountain lions, also viewed the cat as an important symbol. Most active at the borders between night and day, and often hunting in prey-rich edge habitats, the mountain lion symbolized to them transitions in both space and time, such as the borders of Inca territory or a young man's passage into manhood.

Many native peoples saw the mountain lion in some sort of relationship with healing, illness, or death. In Navajo sand paintings, mountain lions are sometimes shown bringing gifts of medicinal herbs. The Apaches and Hualpais believed that a mountain lion's wailing cry foretold death, and their healers sometimes dangled a dried mountain lion paw over the head of a sick person to drive out the evil causing the illness. The Havasupais used mountain lion gall to give an ailing person strength.

Along with their paws and gall, other parts of the mountain lion have been used for various purposes. Gold-ornamented mountain lion skins, skulls intact, were draped over participants in various Inca ceremonies. Mountain lion skins were made into saddle blankets by the Lakota. Many native people made quivers from mountain lion skin, perhaps with the hope of imparting to their arrows the stealth and strength of the cat. Claws became necklaces and tails decorated clothing. Some groups also ate the flesh of the mountain lion.

Despite their sometimes bad reputation and their ceremonial usefulness, mountain lions were not hunted in any great numbers by the native peoples of America. It would take the arrival of the Europeans with their different lifestyle and values to begin the organized slaughter of the great cats.

CIVILIZING THE WILDERNESS

From the fireside stories of the first explorers and settlers, a mythical mountain lion arose—an evil, bloodthirsty creature who would snatch a child from its cradle, slaughter a herd of cows, or kill for the sheer joy of inflicting terror. With these tales as their guide, early homesteaders killed mountain lions to protect their families and the livestock on which their survival depended.

As small settlements began to expand and people began to push farther into the wilderness, forests were cleared and wild animals were killed or forced out. The overwhelming attitude was one of conquest and expansion, driven by the fuel of manifest destiny. In the clear vision of hindsight, the results were predictable.

By the turn of the century, the mountain lion and other predators were virtually wiped out in the eastern United States, as were the once abundant herds of deer that had provided them with food. The tide of humans was moving ever westward, and the real business of predator control was about to get under way.

PREDATOR CONTROL

Bounties on mountain lions can be traced back to the early days of settlement. In 1694, Connecticut paid twenty shillings each for dead "catamounts." By 1742, Massachusetts was paying forty shillings apiece, and in 1753, the amount increased to four pounds. The bounty business continued to grow, finally exploding into a major assault on all predators at the beginning of the twentieth century.

In 1899, hunters hired by the federal government began killing mountain lions in Yellowstone National Park to protect the mountain sheep and elk herds. This developed into a plan to completely eliminate the cat from the park—a plan that worked so well that by 1914 the elk herd was much too large to be supported by its range. Starvation and disease claimed many in 1919–20; the effects of removing their predators were still evident by the winter of 1961–62, when almost five thousand elk were shot to save them from the same fate.

In 1915, in response to pressure from stockmen and sportsmen, the U.S. Congress became a wildlife manager, appropriating money for predator control and charging the predecessor of the U.S. Fish and Wildlife Service (USFWS), the U.S. Biological Survey, with the mission of eliminating undesirable animals, mainly wolves and coyotes. The Animal Damage Control Act of 1931 expanded the hit list, granting authorization and funding for the extermination of "mountain lions, wolves, coyotes, bobcats, prairie dogs, gophers, ground squirrels, jackrabbits, and other animals injurious to agriculture, horticulture, forestry, husbandry, game, or domestic animals, or that carried disease."

Between the federal money, state bounties, and extra incentives paid by counties and stockmen's associations, a professional hunter could now make a good living killing mountain lions, earning as much as $629 per cat. Hunting with dogs was the favored method, but traps and poisoned bait were also used. Some of the hunters became legendary: Ben Lilly, Charles Jesse Jones, and J. T. Owens are credited with killing more than a thousand mountain lions each. J. T. Owens also had the dubious honor of being a lead player in one of the most classic examples of wildlife mismanagement ever seen.

In 1908, Owens was hired to kill mountain lions and other predators in the Kaibab Forest game preserve in Arizona in order to protect the deer there. He did his job so well that by 1919 the deer herd in the preserve had far outstripped the carrying capacity of their range. In 1924, seventeen hundred deer were counted in a single meadow. Every winter saw thousands die from starvation and disease, until finally hunters were allowed in to reduce herd numbers—something that

almost certainly wouldn't have been necessary had the predators been allowed to remain.

Did we learn from Yellowstone and Kaibab? Maybe, but the same error has been repeated many times on a smaller scale. Predator control bounties continued through the 1960s, with Arizona paying until 1971. Ronald Nowak of the USFWS determined that a minimum of 66,667 mountain lions were killed in the United States and Canada between 1907 and 1978.

33

The bounties may be gone, but predator control continues. Hunters working for Animal Damage Control (ADC), a branch of the U.S. Department of Agriculture, kill thousands of animals every year, including mountain lions. Large sums of money are involved in this program, although, as wildlife biologist Kevin Hansen points out, the economics are questionable. According to Hansen, California spent $3.2 million in 1988 to kill 32,368 mammals (including 41 mountain lions) that were considered responsible for a total of $1.4 million estimated damage to livestock, poultry, and crops. It would have cost half as much to simply compensate the farmers and ranchers for their losses. In 1990, Hansen adds, ADC spent $29.4 million in federal funds plus about $15 million in state money to slaughter birds and mammals classed as undesirable pests or predators. Clearly, there are strong forces behind the continued funding of this program.

Some livestock producers still advocate killing mountain lions and other predators as a way of reducing livestock losses. Although mountain lions are responsible for only a very small percentage of total livestock losses, the effect of a depredating cat can be significant to ranchers within its range. Cattle are usually taken as calves, which are most vulnerable when cows are calving in mountain lion habitat. Sheep suffer their greatest losses when they are spread out on the rangeland during the summer. Sometimes a mountain lion kills far more animals than it can eat, a behavior known as surplus killing. This is probably a natural reaction to encountering a concentrated group of prey animals that don't flee as they normally would. Nevertheless, this behavior can leave behind a pile of carcasses and a rancher with an understandable desire for revenge.

Unfortunately, the traditional solutions to the depredation problem, eliminating or reducing mountain lion populations, are usually ineffective as long-term solutions. New Mexico tried on three separate occasions to exterminate mountain lions from problem zones without showing any significant decrease in depredation rates. If the habitat is suitable for mountain lions, vacant home ranges will soon be filled with transients. Livestock losses may actually increase if the transients, who are likely to be still developing hunting skills and learning about local prey populations, turn to the easier fare provided by domestic stock.

One of the alternate solutions has been to change livestock management practices. Two methods that have been effective in reducing depredation are pasturing animals in areas that offer less cover for the mountain lions, and changing from sheep

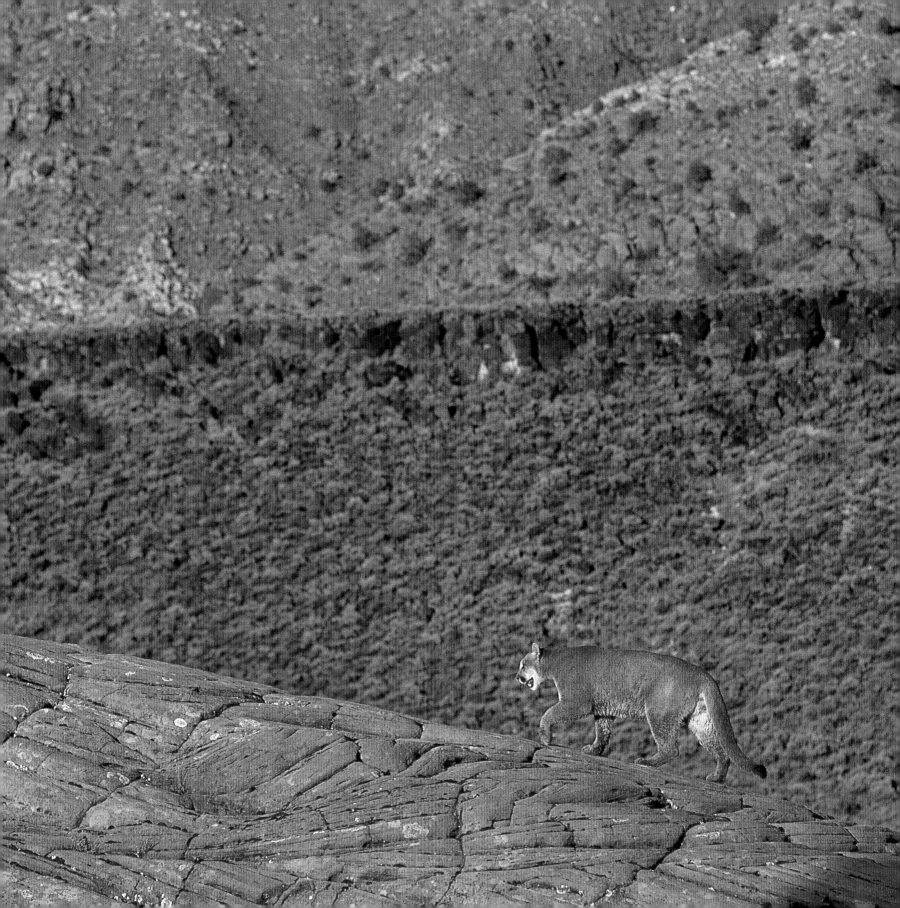

or cow-calf to steer operations in areas of heavy losses. However, discussions about depredation and predator control still turn into acrimonious arguments, and there appears to be little overall change in the rule of thumb used by stock producers in lion country: a dead mountain lion doesn't kill livestock.

SPORT HUNTING

Government agents and stock producers aren't the only ones stalking mountain lions. Each year, hunters looking for trophies make their contribution to the kill figures. Hunting mountain lions for sport has a long tradition. Around the turn of the century, it was a fashionable sport for privileged men from the Northeast. Theodore Roosevelt, a typical example of the hunter-naturalist of the day, spent five weeks in Colorado in 1901, during which he and his companions killed fourteen mountain lions. One of them, a male weighing 227 pounds and measuring eight feet from nose to tail tip, had the unhappy distinction of being the very first record

of the Boone and Crockett Club, which to this day keeps the official scorecard of best trophy kills of various species.

Guiding hunters who want to kill mountain lions has become a booming business. Using expensive, well-trained dogs equipped with radio collars to aid in locating them, outfitters drive the roads looking for mountain lion tracks, especially after a fresh snowfall. Once tracks are found, the dogs are pointed in the right direction and released. When tracks are discovered in the snow and the hunter has reasonably competent dogs, it is highly likely a mountain lion will be treed. At this point, the hunter simply puts a load in the chamber, walks up, lifts the gun, and shoots the mountain lion as it sits in the tree. Eventually a taxidermist may mount the skin in a suitably ferocious snarling pose, demonstrating for the hunter's friends the great bravery that was needed to face down such a dangerous adversary.

The majority of outfitters and guides are responsible, following with their client close behind the dogs. But less reputable outfitters use the advantages of today's

technology in ways that bear no conceivable connection to sport hunting. Mercury switches placed on the dogs' collars are tripped and send a signal when the dog lifts its head into a vertical position, as it does when barking at a mountain lion in a tree above its head. The hunter then has no need to follow the dogs at all but can simply sit in the truck monitoring the receiver and wait until a cat is treed. Even worse are the "will-call" operations, in which outfitters tree a mountain lion, then phone a distant client, who flies out to bag his trophy. This can mean keeping the cat treed for a day or two until the shooter arrives. Most states have laws against keeping a mountain lion treed overnight, but it still happens.

Sport hunting of mountain lions was banned in California in 1990, and the ban was upheld by popular vote in 1996. The states of Washington, Oregon, Montana, Arizona, Colorado, Idaho, Nevada, New Mexico, and Wyoming and the provinces of Alberta and British Columbia all allow trophy hunting during specified seasons with some restrictions. Texas, clinging to a frontier mentality with respect to predators, considers mountain lions to be varmints and keeps a completely open season, with no bag limit and no regulations against shooting females or cubs.

The question of how sport hunting affects mountain lion populations is open for debate. Population figures tend to be far from well known, which is not surprising given the cat's secretive ways. In addition, the effect of hunting depends not only on how many mountain lions

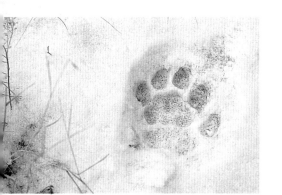

are killed but also on their sex and age. For example, killing female mountain lions removes both them and their future offspring from the population. Unrecorded kills add yet another unknown to the equation. And the thriving black market in trophy animals and supposedly medicinal body parts is putting tremendous pressure on wildlife around the world, including mountain lions.

Our best information appears to indicate that, in some areas at least, mountain lion populations seem able to withstand relatively high losses. However, our best information isn't always very good, particularly when it comes to counting mountain lions. We do know that one source of pressure on existing populations—habitat loss—is increasing. Therefore, it would seem prudent to err on the side of caution when setting sport hunting quotas and depredation permit numbers, especially in areas where the population figures are known to be questionable. It is an exceptionally poor strategy to wait until an animal population is known to be in trouble before practicing species preservation.

There is, of course, a facet of the sport hunting issue that may be overlooked in all the fuss over population numbers. Regardless of how many mountain lions there are, is it right to kill any one of them purely to satisfy the desire for a trophy? Should the fact that their species is not classified as endangered provide sufficient excuse to treat an animal as a target provided for human amusement?

THE SITUATION TODAY

Mountain lions are appearing in the media with increasing frequency. The trophy hunting debate continues to spark ballot initiatives favoring one side or the other. Two other issues generating interest in the big cats are a growing number of mountain lion attacks on humans and the plight of some mountain lion subspecies, including the Florida panther.

MOUNTAIN LION ATTACKS

Paul Beier, who made a landmark study of all documented mountain lion attacks on humans occurring in the United States and Canada from 1890 to 1990, noted that more people die each year from attacks by dogs or rattlesnakes than were killed over that hundred-year period by mountain lions. Although the chance of being killed by a mountain lion is also far less than that of being struck by lightning or even dying from a bee sting, the panic generated by a single attack can be enormous, leading to lawsuits against parks and calls for mountain lion extermination. This panic has gained strength from a marked increase in attacks in recent years, with more attacks occurring between 1970 and 1990 than had taken place in the eighty preceding years. The reasons for this trend are a point of debate.

"If you don't hunt them, they lose their fear of humans!" cry the hunters, pointing to increased attacks in California since the ban of sport hunting. However, Vancouver Island, British Columbia, where mountain lions are heavily hunted, has the highest concentrations of attacks. No one knows why this is, but one theory speculates that hunters kill the most passive mountain lions; those mountain lions aggressive enough to attack pursuing dogs escape to reproduce, thus eventually selectively breeding for aggressive behavior. Or perhaps Vancouver Island mountain lions have different learned behaviors or have more difficulty obtaining enough food while they develop their hunting skills because of the island's lack of small game.

There are probably two main causes for the increase in attacks on Vancouver Island and elsewhere: more and more people are pushing farther into the wild areas that mountain lions call home, and there may be more mountain lions out there looking for space because of changes in hunting policies. The majority of attacks happen at the edges of civilization, where wildlands meet suburbia. There also seems to be a problem with humans believing in a sanitized version of the great outdoors, failing to respect the wild in wildlife. Common sense would suggest that anyone spending time in the wilderness should be aware of the hazards, one of which is encountering potentially dangerous animals.

An agile leap carries this mountain lion over a dangerous chasm.

A Florida panther. Scientists estimate the Florida panther population to be less than fifty.

bend over or sit down are more likely to be attacked. If you are attacked, fighting back—not running—will give you the best chance of survival.

MOUNTAIN LIONS IN TROUBLE

Some subspecies of *Puma concolor* have been so greatly reduced in numbers that their continuing existence is in question. These include the Florida panther *(P. c. coryi),* the eastern cougar *(P. c. cougar),* the Costa Rica puma *(P. c. costa ricensis),* and, to a lesser extent, the Yuma puma *(P. c. browni)* and the Wisconsin cougar *(P. c. schorgeri).*

The Yuma puma, also known as the Colorado desert lion, and the Wisconsin cougar are given a Category 2 classification by the USFWS, meaning that although information about them is inconclusive, there are reasons to be concerned about their numbers. Scientists are currently performing genetic studies to determine whether the Yuma puma is actually a distinct subspecies. Mountain lion hunting is still allowed in the Yuma puma's range, although these cats cannot be visually

distinguished from their less threatened relatives. On the basis of past experience, officials believe that the exceptionally rugged terrain of the area discourages hunters and offers adequate protection for the cats.

Whether the eastern cougar still exists at all is the subject of continuing controversy. Those that say it does point to large and increasing numbers of sightings, including some by knowledgeable observers, as well as the identification of a resident mountain lion population in Manitoba that appears to be composed of the eastern subspecies. In 1993, mountain lion tracks and scat (feces) were identified in New Brunswick. The naysayers' best rebuttal lies in the findings of an intensive five-year study that covered Georgia, South Carolina, North Carolina, Tennessee, and Virginia, an area that overlaps the ranges of both the eastern cougar and the Florida panther. Robert Downing, the biologist in charge of the project, reported that not one reliable sign of a mountain lion's presence was found, even when searching in snowy conditions under which western

Because areas of human settlement are expanding, the potential for human/mountain lion encounters will continue to increase. Being aware of the mountain lion's presence, and understanding its habits and needs, can help reduce the risk of these meetings becoming deadly. It is important not to leave children unsupervised— Beier noted that most mountain lion attack victims were children playing alone or with other children. Standing upright is also a good idea. Small children and adults who studies had 100 percent success in finding tracks. In the study area at least, the eastern cougar appeared to be only a memory. Downing wrote the proposal for an eastern cougar recovery plan, required by the Endangered Species Act, placing first priority on finding cats, but no official action was taken. Reported sightings continue, however, and clearly we need additional thorough searches to either confirm or deny the cat's existence before we can make intelligent decisions about land use in potential eastern cougar habitats.

THE FLORIDA PANTHER

Originally found from eastern Texas to South Carolina, by the 1890s, when hunter-naturalist Charles Cory described the cat that would later bear his name, the Florida panther was already disappearing. By 1946, the range of the panther, as described in Young and Goldman's classic work, *The Puma: Mysterious American Cat,* was limited to isolated pockets in southern Florida. In the 1950s, Florida became one of the first states to pass legislation protecting the mountain lion, and the cat gained further protection when it was listed as an endangered subspecies under the Endangered Species Act in 1973. Today, however, despite decades of protection, the total population of Florida panthers is believed to be only thirty to fifty cats.

One of the reasons for the Florida panthers' incredible decline was heavy hunting of their main food sources, white-tailed deer and feral hogs. This reached a peak in the early 1940s, when a drive to exterminate the deer, because they carried ticks that caused cattle fever, reduced deer numbers to such an extent that they all but disappeared from the landscape. Some authorities feel that only the presence of feral hogs kept the panthers from being starved into extinction at that point. Deer were eventually restocked, but heavy sport hunting of both deer and hogs kept prey numbers down. However, the biggest problem with hunting seemed to be the disruptive presence of humans with their dogs and vehicles in panther habitats. Protecting the panthers, without safeguarding them from human encroachment, just wasn't working. Finally, despite vociferous objections from deer and hog hunters, the Florida Game and Fresh Water Fish Commission banned the use of hunting dogs, reduced the length of the hunting season, designed a trail system that avoided the best areas for panther dens and daytime resting spots, and initiated a permit system for the offroad vehicles used by hunters.

The other major problem for the Florida panther is the loss, fragmentation, and, some say, mismanagement of their habitat. Growing populations and expanding agricultural operations have gobbled up Florida land at an incredible rate. Setting land aside for wildlife is always a hot issue, and when land prices rise, tempers escalate as well. Both the federal government and the state of Florida have adopted an aggressive attitude toward expanding public land holdings, making at least some gains in habitat preservation. But the problem isn't going away. The two main causes of death in the small remaining panther population are road fatalities and intraspecies aggression—both clear indications of the fragmented and insufficient nature of the habitat now available to the cats. Panthers wishing to establish home ranges must run a gauntlet of highway traffic or fight a resident cat for possession of its range. This is leading to deaths the small population can ill afford.

The reduced size of the panther population has raised grave concerns that it may not be genetically viable—that it is too inbred to save. Problems rarely seen in other wild cat populations, such as malformed sperm and cardiac defects, show up with alarming regularity in Florida panthers. However, there may be a cause other than inbreeding for these problems: hormone-disrupting estrogenic compounds.

The environment in which the Florida panther lives is known to be contaminated with a witches' brew of toxins, including mercury and various persistent pesticide residues. Recent research, including several studies described by Theo Colborn et al. in *Our Stolen Future,* has revealed that some of these chemicals appear to fool an animal's hormone system into believing that they are estrogen, and they can appar-

ently have significant effects on fetuses in the womb that later result in reproductive disorders in the mature animal. A study is under way at the National Wildlife Health Center in Madison, Wisconsin, to determine if these compounds are present in Florida panthers.

In order to add new genetic material to the existing Florida panther population, a decision was made in 1994 to begin an outbreeding program by bringing in mountain lions from Texas to mix with the Florida cats. It was felt that since the Florida panther's range had historically met with that of the Texas population, using Texas cats would be the closest thing to a natural mixing of mountain lion populations.

Outbreeding was believed to be more biologically sound and was much less expensive than captive breeding of Florida panthers. Recent results of the program look promising. Of the eight Texas female lions brought to South Florida in 1995, seven were still living at the time of this writing, and they had borne five litters of cubs. The genetic profiles of these off-

spring are helping to define the term Florida panther.

MOUNTAIN LIONS IN THE FUTURE

The biggest threat facing mountain lions, as well as other wildlife, is habitat loss. There is little point in saving species if we don't preserve a place for them to live. Growing human populations with an increasing need for resources have placed even the national parks under pressure to allow development. And the problem is not just direct habitat destruction but the disruptive presence of humans and their various accoutrements.

The Florida panther is barely clinging to survival. It will almost certainly no longer exist as a wild species if more habitat is not made available and protected. Concentrated in one small area, the panthers are vulnerable to disease and natural disaster, and they have no room to expand their numbers even if their reproductive problems can be overcome.

Mountain lions continue to live their lives as they have for thousands of years, adjusting as best they can to the changes

A Florida panther in the Florida Everglades.
Even if the number of Florida panthers
can be increased, substantial steps will need
to be taken to ensure adequate habitat for the
animals to live in.

that humans impose on their world. We must do our best not to push them beyond their abilities to adapt.

Human attitudes toward mountain lions have always been based mainly on guesswork and belief, rather than on fact. Although this was partly due to the mountain lion's secretive habits, which made learning about them difficult, perhaps the main reason lies in the human tendency to designate as "good" or "bad" creatures for whom these terms have no meaning. Whether we venerate them as gods or damn them as evil killers, mountain lions are merely doing what they have evolved to do, living in the only way they know. It is up to us to understand this, to appreciate the role they play in the world, and to take actions that will assure them a place in the future. They have a right to exist in as much solitude as we can give them, and we have a need to know that they are there. For, as our own lives grow increasingly crowded and stressful, there is a quiet peace in knowing that somewhere mountain lions continue to walk alone—silent, elegant, and elusive.

These books are a good place to begin:

ALVAREZ, KEN. *TWILIGHT OF THE PANTHER: BIOLOGY, BUREAUCRACY AND FAILURE IN AN ENDANGERED SPECIES PROGRAM*. SARASOTA, FL: MYAKKA RIVER PUBLISHING, 1993.
An interesting look at the Florida panther and the politics behind protecting it.

HANSEN, KEVIN. *COUGAR: THE AMERICAN LION*. FLAGSTAFF, AZ: NORTHLAND PUBLISHING, 1992.
A detailed, current reference.

YOUNG, STANLEY P., AND EDWARD A. GOLDMAN. *THE PUMA: MYSTERIOUS AMERICAN CAT*. NEW YORK: DOVER PUBLICATIONS, 1946.
A classic work loaded with information.

Have a look at this video:

COUGAR: GHOST OF THE ROCKIES. STAMFORD, CT: CAPITAL CITIES/ABC VIDEO PUBLISHING, 1990.
Nicely illustrates the mountain lion's strength and elegance.

Contact these organizations for information on how you can help mountain lions:

MOUNTAIN LION FOUNDATION, P.O. BOX 1896, SACRAMENTO, CA 95812, (916) 442-2666.

HORNOCKER WILDLIFE INSTITUTE, INC., P.O. BOX 3246, MOSCOW, ID 83843-1908, (208) 885-6871.

45

*Its actions reminiscent of a housecat,
a mountain lion sharpens its claws
on a log.*

*The fur of these young cubs still
shows traces of their baby markings.*

Mountain lions occupy a wide
variety of habitats from sea level to
mountainside, from rainforest
to desert.

52

A consummate carnivore, the mountain lion relies on excellent vision to locate prey, and strong muscles to capture and kill it.

FOLLOWING PAGES:
An adult mountain lion patrols its home range, the area where it lives and hunts. Possession of a home range is so necessary for survival that females may delay breeding until they have one.

PRECEDING PAGES:

When a male and a female lion
come together to mate, the process
is not always a friendly one.

OPPOSITE:

Still enclosed in its amniotic sac,
a newborn cub gasps for its first breath.

Newborn mountain lion cubs begin
to nurse as their mother licks
them clean. Her tongue, used so
gently now, is very rough and strong
enough to rasp meat from bone.

PRECEDING PAGES:

After the exertion of giving birth, a new

mother rests with her suckling cubs.

A female and her young family enjoy

the cool shade in the shelter of

their den. The cubs will grow quickly

on the extremely rich milk their

mother provides.

The small spotted faces and baby

blue eyes of these young cubs

bear little resemblance to those of

an adult mountain lion.

65

At first on wobbly legs but soon with a bouncing stride, a young mountain lion eagerly explores the area around its den.

66

Dangling limply from its mother's jaws, a small mountain lion gets a ride to a new location. Mountain lion families may change dens several times.

FOLLOWING PAGES:

Female mountain lions are tolerant parents who appear to enjoy the time they spend with their cubs. After allowing herself to be stalked and pummelled by her playful offspring, this mother enjoys a brief respite while the cubs recharge their batteries.

A young lion takes a swat at a tempting target, displaying the strong forepaws that are already beginning to develop into a hunter's deadly weapons.

A rocky shelf provides a good place to rest and soak up the sun.

Ears flat, mouth agape, hissing and snarling, a mountain lion expresses its displeasure.

A mountain lion cub gives its wet

paw a vigorous shake.

Comfortably warm in its fur, a male

mountain lion acquires a blanket

of snow.

Obvious landmarks like this big tree are popular spots for mountain lions to leave scent marks of urine and feces. These signs tell other mountain lions that the area is occupied as well as how recently the owner visited the spot.

FOLLOWING PAGES:

A mountain lion alertly focusses

its attention on something that has

caught its eye.

Mountain lion cubs stay with their
mother for up to two years after
they are born. Having large cubs to
feed through the winter can put a
heavy burden on the hunting female.

Male mountain lions are believed to spend much of their time seeking females that are ready to breed. As it travels through its home range, which may overlap those of several females, the male checks urine left by the females for signs of this readiness.

84

Where they are plentiful, mule deer are a mainstay of mountain lion diets.

The powerful muscles of the hindquarter propel a mountain lion in its final lunge toward its prey. The cat possesses great speed but its small lungs limit the distance it can run before tiring to a few hundred yards.

A deer can provide several meals
for a mountain lion. The lion may
kill the deer or scavenge deer killed
by other predators or automobiles.
Large prey like this are important
food sources in winter, especially if
a female has cubs to feed.

These cubs had their first taste of meat when they were about six weeks old, but they still have some difficulty dealing with a carcass.

After eating its fill, a mountain lion often covers a carcass with dirt, leaves, or, in this case, snow. This may help to conceal it from scavengers until the cat returns for another meal.

PRECEDING PAGES:

Mountain lions can give birth during
any month of the year although
each region has seasons where births
are more plentiful.

A full grown male mountain lion may weigh as much as 180 pounds and measure 8 feet from nose to end of tail. Females are smaller, weighing perhaps 130 pounds and reaching 7 feet in length. The largest mountain lions are found in the northernmost and southernmost parts of their geographical range, but size throughout the complete range varies considerably.

A female reaches down to give her
cub a playful pat.

A mountain lion pauses for a drink
while crossing a shallow stream.

FOLLOWING PAGES:
Mountain lions are good swimmers
when they choose to take to the water.

Mountain lions manage to raise families even in apparently inhospitable surroundings. In dry terrain like this, a source of water is essential for survival.

These cubs still have a lot of growing

to do before they are ready for life

on their own.

The rough and tumble games of
young mountain lions serve a very
important purpose. By improving
balance, coordination, and strength,
play helps hone skills necessary
for survival.

FOLLOWING PAGES:
Small lions in a big world, this pair
of cubs is caught in a rare moment
of stillness.

Even for a mountain lion, hunting porcupines is not without risks. The cat's effort may earn it a paw or face full of quills. However, some cats make the prickly prey a regular part of their diet.

PRECEDING PAGES:

A mountain lion explodes in pursuit

of prey.

Agile over rough terrain, a mountain

lion's supple spine and strong

legs allow it to negotiate obstacles

with ease.

112

The jumping ability of mountain lions is remarkable. From a standstill they can leap twenty-five feet forward or jump twelve feet into the air.

Secretive hunters pursuing a lifestyle evolved over millions of years, mountain lions today find themselves in increasing conflict with humans. It is up to humans to find responsible solutions to the problems and to assure mountain lions a place in our future.

ACKERMAN, BRUCE B., FREDERICK G. LINDZEY, AND THOMAS P. HEMKER. "COUGAR FOOD HABITS IN SOUTHERN UTAH." *JOURNAL OF WILDLIFE MANAGEMENT* 48:1 (1984): 147–155.

ALVAREZ, KEN. *TWILIGHT OF THE PANTHER: BIOLOGY, BUREAUCRACY AND FAILURE IN AN ENDANGERED SPECIES PROGRAM.* SARASOTA, FL: MYAKKA RIVER PUBLISHING, 1993.

ANDERSON, ALLEN E. *A CRITICAL REVIEW OF LITERATURE ON PUMA (FELIS CONCOLOR).* COLORADO DIVISION OF WILDLIFE: SPECIAL REPORT NO. 54, 1983.

BARNES, CLAUDE T. *THE COUGAR OR MOUNTAIN LION.* SALT LAKE CITY, UT: RALTON, 1960.

BELDEN, ROBERT C., AND BRUCE W. HAGEDORN. "FEASIBILITY OF TRANS-LOCATING PANTHERS INTO NORTHERN FLORIDA." *JOURNAL OF WILDLIFE MANAGEMENT* 57:2 (1993): 388–397.

BELDEN, ROBERT C., WILLIAM B. FRANKENBERGER, ROY T. MCBRIDE, AND STEPHEN T. SCHWIKERT. "PANTHER HABITAT USE IN SOUTHERN FLORIDA." *JOURNAL OF WILDLIFE MANAGEMENT* 52:4 (1988): 660–663.

BOLGIANO, CHRIS. *MOUNTAIN LION: AN UNNATURAL HISTORY OF PUMAS AND PEOPLE.* MECHANICSBURG, PA: STACKPOLE BOOKS, 1995.

BRANDT, ANTHONY. "LIONS ON THE HAUNT." *OUTDOOR LIFE* 197:1 (1996): 14(4).

BUSCH, ROBERT H. *THE COUGAR ALMANAC.* NEW YORK: LYONS & BURFORD, 1996.

CARROLL, CHRISTINE. "CAT FIGHT." *TEXAS MONTHLY.* 21:6 (1993): 50(7).

CIOTTI, PAUL. "CAT FIGHT." *NATIONAL REVIEW* 46:24 (1994): 24(2).

COLBORN, THEO, DIANNE DUMANOSKI, AND JOHN PETERSON MYERS. *OUR STOLEN FUTURE.* NEW YORK: DUTTON (PENGUIN), 1996.

DOSKOCH, PETER. "COUGARS COME TO TOWN." *SCIENCE WORLD.* 52:1 (1995): 8(4).

EASTMAN, CHARLES A. *RED HUNTERS AND THE ANIMAL PEOPLE.* NEW YORK: HARPER & BROTHERS PUBLISHERS, 1904.

EWER, R. F. *THE CARNIVORES.* ITHACA, NY: CORNELL UNIVERSITY PRESS, 1973.

GARNER, JOE. *NEVER A TIME TO TRUST: A STORY OF BRITISH COLUMBIA, HER PIONEERS, PREDATORS AND PROBLEMS.* NANAIMO, B.C.: CINNABAR PRESS, 1984.

GUGGISBERG, C.A.W. *WILD CATS OF THE WORLD.* NEW YORK: TAPLINGER, 1975.

HANSEN, KEVIN. *COUGAR: THE AMERICAN LION.* FLAGSTAFF, AZ: NORTHLAND PUBLISHING, 1992.

HANSEN, KEVIN. "RETURN OF THE COUGAR." *AMERICAN FORESTS* (101:1–2) (1995): 25(6).

HIBBEN, FRANK C. *HUNTING AMERICAN LIONS.* NEW YORK: THOMAS H. CROWELL, 1948.

HORNOCKER, MAURICE G. "LEARNING TO LIVE WITH MOUNTAIN LIONS." *NATIONAL GEOGRAPHIC* 182:1 (1992): 52–65.

IRIARTE, J. AGUSTIN, WILLIAM L. FRANKLIN, WARREN E. JOHNSON, AND KENT H. REDFORD. "BIOGEOGRAPHIC VARIATION OF FOOD HABITS AND BODY SIZE OF THE AMERICAN PUMA." *OECOLOGIA* 85 (1990): 185–190.

KITCHENER, ANDREW. *THE NATURAL HISTORY OF THE WILD CATS.* ITHACA, NY: COMSTOCK, 1991.

KOEHLER, GARY M., AND MAURICE G. HORNOCKER. "SEASONAL RESOURCE USE AMONG MOUNTAIN LIONS, BOBCATS, AND COYOTES," *JOURNAL OF MAMMALOGY* 72:2 (1991): 391–396.

115

LAWRENCE, R. D. *THE GHOST WALKER.* TORONTO, ON: MCCLELLAND AND STEWART, 1983.

LINDZEY, FREDERICK G., WALTER D. VAN SICKLE, BRUCE W. ACKERMAN, DAN BARNHURST, THOMAS P. HEMKER, AND STEVEN P. LAING. "COUGAR POPULATION DYNAMICS IN SOUTHERN UTAH." *JOURNAL OF WILDLIFE MANAGEMENT.* 58:4 (1994): 619–624.

LINN, AMY. "WILD CATS WILD: WORRYING OVER THE LION'S SHARE OF MONTANA." *AUDUBON* 95:4 (1993): 22(3).

LOGAN, KENNETH A., LARRY L. IRWIN, AND RONELL SKINNER. "CHARACTERISTICS OF A HUNTED MOUNTAIN LION POPULATION IN WYOMING." *JOURNAL OF WILDLIFE MANAGEMENT* 50:4 (1986): 648–654.

LOGAN, KENNETH A., LINDA L. SWEANOR, TONI K. RUTH, AND MAURICE G. HORNOCKER. "COUGARS OF THE SAN ANDRES MOUNTAINS, NEW MEXICO." FINAL REPORT, FEDERAL AID IN WILDLIFE RESTORATION, PROJECT W-128-R. SANTA FE, NM: NEW MEXICO DEPARTMENT OF GAME & FISH, SEPTEMBER 1996.

MAEHR, DAVID S., ROBERT C. BELDEN, E. DARRELL LAND, AND LAURIE WILKINS. "FOOD HABITS OF PANTHERS IN SOUTHWEST FLORIDA." *JOURNAL OF WILDLIFE MANAGEMENT* 54:3 (1990): 420–423.

MCCALL, KAREN, AND JIM DUTCHER. *COUGAR: GHOST OF THE ROCKIES.* VANCOUVER, B.C.: DOUGLAS & MCINTYRE, 1992.

PETERSEN, DAVID. "GHOST OF THE MOUNTAIN." *BACKPACKER* 22:1 (1994): 6(2).

RENNICKE, JEFF. "RETURN OF THE GHOST CAT." *BACKPACKER* 23:4 (1995): 28(4).

ROBINSON, JEROME B. "CAT IN THE BALLOT BOX." *FIELD & STREAM* 100:11 (1996): 30(2).

ROSS, P. IAN, AND MARTIN G. JALKOTZY. "CHARACTERISTICS OF A HUNTED POPULATION OF COUGARS IN SOUTH-WESTERN ALBERTA." *JOURNAL OF WILDLIFE MANAGEMENT* 56:3 (1992): 417–426.

RYCHNOVSKY, RAY, AND DOUG THOMPSON. "CLAWING INTO CONTROVERSY: PROTECTED BY LAW, THE CALIFORNIA MOUNTAIN LION BOLDLY EXPANDS ITS RANGE." *OUTDOOR LIFE* 195:1 (1995): 38(5).

SAVAGE, CANDACE. *WILD CATS: LYNX, BOBCATS, MOUNTAIN LIONS.* VANCOUVER, B.C.: DOUGLAS & MCINTYRE, 1993.

SHAW, HARLEY. *SOUL AMONG LIONS: THE COUGAR AS PEACEFUL ADVERSARY.* BOULDER, CO: JOHNSON, 1989.

TINSLEY, JIM BOB. *THE PUMA: LEGENDARY LION OF THE AMERICAS.* EL PASO, TX: TEXAS WESTERN PRESS, THE UNIVERSITY OF TEXAS AT EL PASO, 1987.

TOOPS, CONNIE. "CATS OF ONE COLOR." *NATIONAL PARKS* 69:7–8 (1995): 30(6).

VAN DYKE, FRED G., RAINIER H. BROCKE, HARLEY G. SHAW, BRUCE B. ACKERMAN, THOMAS P. HEMKER, AND FREDERICK G. LINDZEY. "REACTIONS OF MOUNTAIN LIONS TO LOGGING AND HUMAN ACTIVITY." *JOURNAL OF WILDLIFE MANAGEMENT* 50:1 (1986): 95–102.

WHITE, TOM. *SASKATCHEWAN COUGAR—ELUSIVE CAT.* SPECIAL PUBLICATION NO. 14. REGINA, SK: SASKATCHEWAN NATURAL HISTORY SOCIETY, 1982.

WILLIAMS, TED. "THE LION'S SILENT RETURN." *AUDUBON* 96:6 (1994): 28(7).

WOOD, DANIEL. "COUGARS ON THE REBOUND." *BEAUTIFUL BRITISH COLUMBIA* 38:4 (1996): 20–30.

WRIGHT, BRUCE S. *THE EASTERN PANTHER: A QUESTION OF SURVIVAL.* TORONTO, ON: CLARKE, IRWIN & CO., 1972.

YOUNG, STANLEY P., AND EDWARD A. GOLDMAN. *THE PUMA: MYSTERIOUS AMERICAN CAT.* NEW YORK: DOVER PUBLICATIONS, 1946.

INDEX